THE INVINCIBLE TONY SPEARS

For Tim Peake and Major Tom

HODDER CHILDREN'S BOOKS

First published in Great Britain in 2016

This edition published in 2016 by Hodder & Stoughton

Text and illustrations copyright © 2016 Neal Layton

The moral rights of the author have been asserted.

1 2 3 4 5 6 7 8 9 10

A CIP catalogue record for this book is available from the British Library.

ISBN: 978 1 444 91952 3

Printed and bound in China

The paper and board used in this book are made from wood from responsible sources.

Hodder Children's Books

An imprint of Hachette Children's Group

Part of Hodder & Stoughton

Carmelite House

50 Victoria Embankment

London EC4Y 0DZ

An Hachette UK Company

www.hachette.co.uk

THE INVINCIBLE
TONY SPEARS

Neal Layton

Hodder Children's Books

New
School
tie

NEW
**TOO
BIG**
BLAZER

NEW
STIFF
SCHOOL
TROUSERS

NEW
UNCOMFORTABLE
SCHOOL
SHOES

1. THE BUTTON

Tony Spears didn't feel invincible.

Not one bit.

His mum had got a new job, with better pay, in a better area.

New house, new school, new uniform — it was all too much, and right now Tony couldn't see the 'better' in any of it.

His first day at St John's had started out badly, with the headteacher reminding the school of their fast-approaching 'Annual Best Pupil Award'. What was the point telling Tony about it? Because he had joined the school mid-term he had missed weeks of point giving. So guess how many points he had? Zero. Even the naughtiest kids in the year had some points, maybe one, two, a thousand! – but Tony didn't even have that. Just a big ZERO written next to his name.

The rest of the day

was a blur of places to

go and people,

4

lots and lots of them.

To make matters even worse, his watch broke, so he didn't know the time, and he was late for everything. Finally, after slogging his way through the rest of the day, he found himself walking home alone with a heavy heart, through unfamiliar streets, back to the new flat.

He reached for the key around his neck, opened the door and began to weave his way through the sea of half-unpacked cardboard

boxes towards the kitchen. In their last flat Tony knew where everything was. When he got home from school he would effortlessly move from cupboard to fridge to work surface, munching peanut-butter-honey-jam sandwiches almost as fast as he could make them. But this new kitchen was hopeless. He found the peanut butter but where were the plates?

He tried all the drawers.

Damp matches, string, a cotton reel, bits of paper.

Nope.

Right, cupboards.

Cereal boxes, rice, tennis balls – what were they doing in there?

Nope. Nope. Nope.

Until eventually, in the very last cupboard under the sink he found one tiny dusty plastic saucer that must have belonged to the previous tenants.

It was whilst sifting through this cupboard that Tony Spears found **THE SIGN** and **THE RED BUTTON...**

'The sign' was printed in funny black cut-out stickers. It said:

PRESS THIS BUTTON

TO INITIATE

PROCEDURES FOR

TAKE OFF

and beneath it was a round red button. That's odd, thought Tony. I wonder what it does?

Tony's finger hovered over it for a few seconds, before pushing it down with a satisfying click.

At first nothing happened. Just another thing in this house that doesn't work, thought Tony. Then he began to notice a

LOW RUMBLING NOISE...

Quite suddenly the whole kitchen floor lurched sideways and Tony was thrown from his feet. He had just regained his balance when it moved awkwardly the other way, and with a loud metallic clunk, his stomach began to rise into his throat as if he was falling in an elevator.

'Oh help, what have I done?'

Metal shutters were slowly lowering over all the windows and the door.

Tony began to panic as the rumbling, scraping sound increased. All the kitchen shelves were disappearing into the walls.

The whole room transforming before his eyes until – with another loud clunking noise – Tony was sent sprawling to the ground.

And suddenly silence.

When he picked himself up, he found himself not in his kitchen, but in a glowing white room with a large screen at one end. Several feet back from the screen was a table covered in dials and flashing lights. In front of that was a seat. The whole scene looked like something from the TV except it 'felt' real, in a way that TV didn't. As his hand reached out to touch the table in front of him the screen flickered and an echoey voice said,

'Good afternoon, Master Spears. Where shall I set course for today?'

2. THE INVINCIBLE

'You seem suprised, Master Spears. I do hope
your journey by hyper-lift was not too
difficult. It does become easier the
second time. I sense you would like to be
somewhere different, but I do not know
where. If you are able to advise me I can
begin the necessary travel arrangements.'

'Where am I? What's going on – is this a spaceship?' blurted out Tony.

'That is correct, Master Spears. You are now on board the *Invincible*, a type 1AA vessel, which is capable of planetary, galactic and other forms of dimensional travel. It's —'

'Wow, a spaceship,' mumbled Tony. 'This is awesome! Um, in that case, can I go to …'

Tony thought for a second. Where do spaceships go? Of course – 'The moon!'

'Affirmative, Master Spears. Destination moon! Lift-off in T minus 20 seconds.

'Engines ready. Powering gravity thrusters. Lift-off in T minus 10 seconds. Please take your seat, Master Spears.'

Tony quickly ran to the chair and sat down. Immediately, as he did so, plastic belts whirred out from the chair back, wrapping themselves round his legs and waist and securing him to the seat.

'Viewing Screen activated. Departure hatch ready. Cloaking systems engaged.

'Lift-off in . . .'

5, 4, 3, 2, 1...

The humming sound began to get much louder and the room began to shake. Tony was glad he was strapped into the chair.

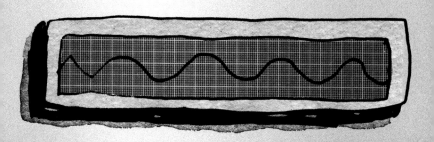

The screen in front of him changed to show lots of blue and white fluffy things that he thought must be clouds. They began to get bigger and bigger until the whole screen went white, then suddenly blue again, darkening to inky black. Stars emerged from the darkness, shooting past like street lights, as gradually, the unmistakable image of the moon began to fill the screen. The whole process hadn't taken more than a minute.

'Wow, that was quick.'

'Yes, Master Spears. The moon is only 384,400 kilometres from Earth, which compared to the size of the universe is nothing.'

Landing didn't take long either. After speeding over the surface the *Invincible* slowed to a stop, hovered and then gently sank down to the dusty floor of a moon crater. It kicked up a tiny bit of dust as its feet made contact with the surface.

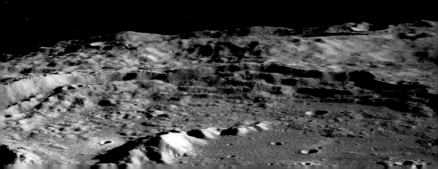

'Touchdown!'

'Woah, this is totally awesome – I've landed on the moon! Quick, let me out. I want to jump around like an astronaut!'

'I'm afraid that is impossible, Master Spears.'

'What?'

'The temperature on the moon varies between minus 153°C in the shade to 123°C in the sun. It also has no atmosphere and is not supportive of human life.'

'OK yeah. I know all that. So get me a space suit like astronauts wear.'

'I'm afraid we do not have any on board. The *Invincible* is designed to only travel to planets capable of supporting human life, of which there are many, more than two billion, to be exact.'

Tony felt anger and resentment well up inside him.

Here I am on the moon, and I can't even get out and jump around like an astronaut. This is so stupid.

'OK, Computer. Where is the nearest

planet that *is* capable of supporting human life? One that I can get out on and explore ...'

'The nearest planet that is suitable for human life forms is called Xo49p.'

'Right, my new destination is planet Xo49p. Let's go – no, wait a minute.'

Settling himself back into the flight chair, Tony noticed some controls which looked like a steering wheel.

'Can I fly there myself?'

'Yes, that is possible though not advisable.'

'Well, I want to.'

'Is that an order, Master Spears?'

'Yes. That is an order!'

'Affirmative, Master Spears. Manual systems engaged.'

Tony gripped the steering wheel. It felt just like ones he'd used on Galaxoids. Beside his right hand was a lever. Now, if this is anything

like playing Galaxoids this should control the engines, he thought. Pushing the lever forward, Tony immediately felt himself rock back into the chair.

'Woah yeah, here we go.'

Stars began zipping past the screen. Turning the steering wheel left and right, he could feel the ship swinging from side to side.

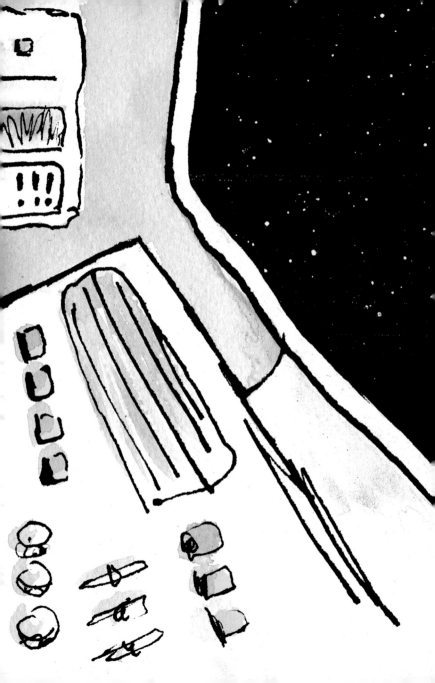

'This *is* just like Galaxoids!' he exclaimed. Pushing the throttle further forward he felt the increased acceleration squeeze him further back in the chair.

'Master Spears, it is not a good idea to continue at this speed. I estimate the chances of a collision to be 45%.'

Tony kept pushing the throttle.

'A what?' said Tony.

'A crash, Master Spears! Please desist from this action. Crash probability is now 69% ... 79% ... 89%...'

But Tony wasn't listening. He was having too much fun, swinging the controls left and right, dodging the dots of light whizzing past, until suddenly one of them went from being

tiny to filling the screen entirely, and with a deafening,

CRUNCHING ROAR.

The whole room shook so violently that Tony was almost thrown from his seat. Then darkness.

Opening his eyes, he gradually felt the shaking subside. Lights started coming on and the screen flickered into life once more.

'Wh-at happened?' mumbled Tony in a shaky voice.

'You crashed head-on into an asteroid the size of Jupiter at a speed of a zillion space miles a second.'

'But … But … I'm OK. Is the ship OK?'

'You are fine, Master Spears, and the ship is fine too.'

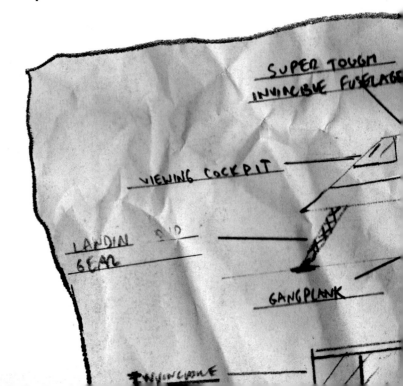

SUPER TOUGH
INVINCIBLE FUSELAGE

VIEWING COCKPIT

LANDIN
GEAR

GANGPLANK

INVINCIBLE

'But how? Shouldn't we be dead or something?'

'Master Spears, you are on board the *Invincible*. It was given that name for a reason. Its hull cannot be damaged by impact,

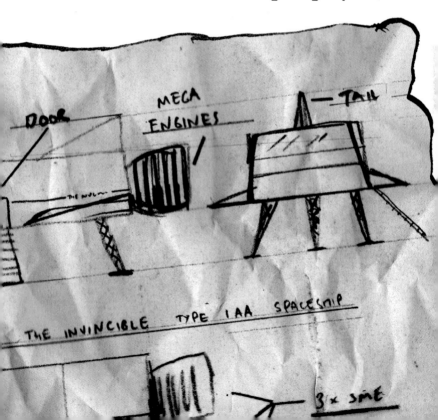

DOOR

MEGA ENGINES

TAIL

THE HULL

THE INVINCIBLE TYPE I.AA SPACESHIP

3 x SME

heat or explosions. It is, as its name implies, totally invincible. Once on board, as long as all windows and doors are secured, you are perfectly safe. I think perhaps we should disengage manual controls for now.'

'Y-yes,' mumbled Tony.

'Automatic systems engaged. Resuming previous orders. Estimated arrival T minus 3 minutes.'

And whilst Tony sat in a somewhat dazed state the computer navigated to Xo49p, the closest planet to Earth suitable for sustaining human life.

Lost in his thoughts, Tony didn't notice the ship's engines change from superfast to landing mode. Or even the gentle bump as all three feet made contact with the soft soil. In fact, it was only when the airlock door hiss-clunked open that Tony realised he had arrived. The safety harness whirred back into the seat and

he turned to see rolling green hills and flowers outside.

The flowers were bigger and brighter than any Tony had ever seen before. They looked beautiful, but it was the smell drifting in that drew Tony outside. Tony got up and started sniffing his way towards the open door. It couldn't be – surely … but it was. The whole planet smelt of bubblegum, of PINK BUBBLEGUM!

3. PLANET Xo49p

By now Tony had made his way through the airlock, down the gangplank and was padding across the soft grass. It was so perfect it looked just like a green carpet.

Then Tony noticed a rustling in the bushes. He froze and suddenly felt like he was not alone. Hairs stood up on the back of his neck. He felt like he was being watched. His ears strained for the smallest possible sound. Then he heard a tiny but unmistakable 'squeeeeeek!'

Looking down, he realised he definitely was not alone, because peering out from behind the bush beside him was a very strange creature. It had two very long ears and looked a bit like a rabbit, only it was larger, fluffier and pinker.

Tony stood riveted to the spot whilst the creature began to walk towards him.

'Do not be afraid. We mean you no harm.'

Tony went very dry in the mouth, unable to speak …

'My name is Plumpy.'

As the creature spoke, all the brightly coloured plants began rustling, as more and more of the creatures appeared from behind leaves, flowers and clumps of grass.

'Whaaat?' exclaimed Tony.

'Do you mean, what *are* we?' asked the creature who had introduced himself as Plumpy.

'We are Squggles, of course! We live on the planet Xo49p, the planet you landed on.'*

---

* A note on how to pronounce Squggles. This is a very difficult word for Earth people to say: there is no equivalent sound in any Earth language. The closest approximation we can make is Skw'ggles.

'Hello! Hello! Hello!' they each said in turn as they greeted Tony. 'And Welcome.'

'Wow,' said Tony. 'This is totally crazy. I've just met some aliens, and they're pink and they look like soft toys!'

Tony gathered his thoughts a little.

'So you live on this planet. Does anything else live on this planet with you? I mean, are there any other alien creatures living here?'

ALIEN LIFEFORM

NO. 5,401

THINGAMAJIG

FUR

HAIR

FLUFF

LOTS MORE
FUR

ALIEN LIFEFORM

NO. 5,402

BIGTUMMYUS

QUITE
BIG
EARS

ENORMOUS
TUMMY

ALIEN LIFEFORM

NO. 5,403

HUMAN

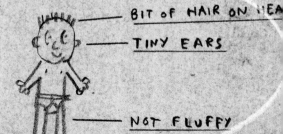

BIT OF HAIR ON HEAD

TINY EARS

NOT FLUFFY

'Firstly we are not aliens, as I'm afraid you are the alien here, Tony. Looking at your lack of fur, skinny tummy and tiny ears I'm guessing you must be a human from the planet Earth.'

'Um y-yes I am,' stuttered Tony.

'But yes,' continued Plumpy. 'Unfortunately there is another animal that lives here. They are called—' and at this point he lowed his voice to a whisper. 'They are called—'

Plumpy never finished his sentence as suddenly Squggles started running away in all directions, and Plumpy with them.

As he ran off Plumpy looked over his shoulder and just had time to shout,

'Gatorillas!'

'You what?' said Tony.

'Gatorillaaaaaas! Run,
Tony, RUN for your LIFE!'

And he was gone.

Tony turned around slowly to look in the
direction Plumpy had been pointing.

Several metres behind him was a huge, hairy gorilla-like animal; gorilla-like except for its head, which was like a crocodile's, and its feet, which were like the talons of an eagle. It was snapping its jaws and running on all fours like an ape, very fast, in Tony's direction.

'Aghhh!' shouted Tony, sprinting after the Squggles as fast as he could.

A little way ahead, set into a bank of luminous grass, were lots of little holes, a bit

like rabbit holes
on Earth. The Squggles
started hoppping down them.
Tony darted towards the
biggest one, throwing himself
down it head first.

He started wriggling. It was just
about big enough to fit him. He managed
to get most of himself underground when the

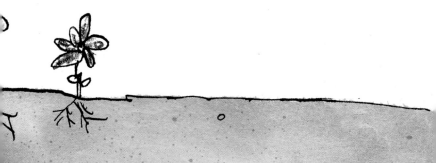

hole began to narrow a little, and then a little bit more, until he became firmly stuck with just his feet poking out, like a cork stuck in a bottle.

Kicking wildly, the more he wriggled the more wedged in he became, and with his hands pinned down beside his body, he couldn't push himself back out.

The Gatorilla must have reached his legs by now. He could almost feel it opening its toothy jaws, about to bit them off, when suddenly he felt lots of furry little hands grabbing his face, hair, ears, nose and teeth, yanking him

POP like a tooth, down under the

ground into the dark.

Down,

down,

down

he fell, spinning round and round until he shot out,

landing with a bump into an enormous brightly lit cavern.

4. FUZZY-SQUGGLE WORLD

Tony sat there blinking, his face dirty and scratched, spitting out mud, taking in his dazzling new surroundings. This is what he saw …

'Hello, Tony'

'Hello. Hello.'

'And welcome.'

The Squggles started crowding round him,
checking him over. Most of them had bumps
and scuffs and were covered in mud too.

'Tony, it's me, Plumpy. Are you OK?
Nobody has ever come down that fast to
Squggle World, and certainly never head first!
Are your legs still there? The Gatorilla didn't
bite them off, did he?'

Tony was pleased to find that his legs were still there and it was then that he noticed something very strange about the Squggles. When they spoke to him, although they looked at him, they didn't move their mouths. In fact, it didn't look like their mouths could move at all. He was just about to say something about it when Plumpy spoke:

'That's right, Tony. We don't move our mouths when we speak. In fact, we don't make any sounds at all, not the way you humans do. You see, we speak telepathically, mind to mind.'

As Plumpy spoke, Tony realised the words were popping straight into his head, almost like he'd thought them himself, but they were in Plumpy's voice.

'But that's enough of me speaking, telepathically or not. You are our guest here. Come, you must be hungry.'

As they walked, and Plumpy talked, Tony marvelled at the underground world where the Squggles lived. Although they were small, soft and furry, everything they had built around them was tall and angular, made of strange shiny materials that Tony had never seen before.

'And this is our Centre for Science. All of our new inventions are developed here, which is next door to the Grand Central Library and the Hall of Really Tricky Mathematics . . .

'Finally, we are arriving at the play park. Have a seat and I'll get you some refreshments. Cyber juice and galactic biscuits, OK?'

As Tony ate, Plumpy introduced him to his friends, Squinky, Jubbly, Snuggy and many more.

Plumpy told him all about fuzzy Squggles, and their life underground on planet Xo49p.

'We don't get many visitors,' he said. 'Most think because we're pink and fluffy we must be stupid, or they get eaten by Gatorillas. Or sometimes both.

'It was the Gatorillas that forced us to live underground, you see. We'd much rather be playing above ground in the flowers, but we're scared. We are their main source of food. We eat cyber juice and galactic biscuits, and they eat us.'

Tony told them all about his new school, his new house and how he came to their planet by spaceship. The Squggles listened intently, but it was when he talked about the *Invincible* that they became very excited.

'Tony, if we could develop something invincible on our planet, we might at last be safe from the Gatorillas. Do you think you could show us your spaceship, so that we might learn from it?'

How could he refuse? They had saved his life. And just given him a lovely snack.

Minutes later, Tony found himself in a lift going back up to the surface. Plumpy had assembled a crack team of the most highly trained operatives for the mission.

They were all dressed in camouflage-patterned dungarees, with tiny helmets, boots and gloves. Some of them had muddy-coloured facepaint.

OUR MISSION: We will get you safely to your spaceship and as we understand it, once inside, as long as the doors and windows are closed, we will be safe to study it. We will then leave you on board and make our way back to Squggle World with the necessary information for constructing something invincible of our own. Tony, I can't thank you enough for this.

There was a pinging noise and a bump. The lift had arrived at ground level.

'Some days we don't have any trouble from the Gatorillas at all,' said Plumpy, 'and we are free to gambol above ground, but that attack earlier today must mean the Gatorillas are hungry, and judging by the ferocity of that attack, today they are *very* hungry. We must be on high alert.'

The lift doors slid open.

'Right, team. Let's go!'

Two of the team immediately scampered out of the lift and hid behind the nearest bush.

'Bush clear. Go, go, GO!'

And in this way they made their way from bush, to flower, to rock, to grassy knoll.

'Down on your bellies. Wriggle through the grass. Go, go, GO!'

Until they were within sight of the *Invincible*. Tony had forgotten his fears of a Gatorilla attack and was actually beginning to enjoy himself.

'Don't worry, as soon as we're inside we'll be safe. It's invincible,' Tony said proudly.

Scanning the area, Tony couldn't see
any sign of Gatorillas. Tentatively, he started
walking across the grassy lawn towards the
spaceship, gaining confidence with every step.

'Look, everyone, there's no one here. The
Gatorillas have gone.'

'Tony, do not make any noise. It's what
alerts the Gatorillas to our presence. It's why
we don't make any—'

'Noise?' questioned Tony. 'Look, I'm
almost at the spaceship and there's nothing.'

He stopped mid-sentence. Climbing onto
the roof of the *Invincible* was not one, but at
least seventeen Gatorillas.

'RUN!' shouted Tony at the top of his
voice. 'Gatorilla attack!'

He was almost at the spaceship so began sprinting up the gangplank. Squggles scattered everywhere, chased by snapping, clawing Gatorillas.

Tony dived through the bulkhead doors and airlock shouting, 'Computer, shut doors immediately … We're under ATTACK!'

The hull doors and airlock closed with a hiss-clunk sound.

Tony was sweating and out of breath.

The computer screen flickered into life, pulsing gently. Waiting for Tony to say something.

'Are the doors secured?'

'Yes, Master Spears.'

'Are the Squggles OK? I mean, have they been eaten?'

'It's not possible to say exactly, Master Spears, but it seems that most of the Squggles made it to safety, though possibly not all of them.'

That was so stupid of me, thought Tony. After all the help they gave me, this is how I repay them.

He lay on his back on the floor. Gathering his breath and feeling very sorry for himself.

As he did so his eye fell upon a flashing panel on the wall. It said Earth Time: 17.05.

'Five past five,' he blurted out.

'Computer, is that the time? What happened?'

'Well, Master Spears, you have travelled two hundred and sixty thousand miles to the moon, and a further hundred and seventeen-zillion-squillion space miles to the planet Xo49p, not counting the time spent drinking juice and eating galactic biscuits.'

'Get me home fast,' said Tony. 'My mum gets back in five minutes. I need to tidy the kitchen and be home in time for tea!'

'It will take at least twenty minutes to travel safely back.'

'No good. I've got to be back in five minutes, or even four minutes.'

'But, Master Spears, travelling and landing at such speed should only be done in an emergency . . .'

'This *is* an emergency. I totally need to go home for my tea. Do it now, please – that's an order.'

'Are you sure, Master Spears?'

'Yes yes, do it.'

'The probability of damage will be significantly increased.'

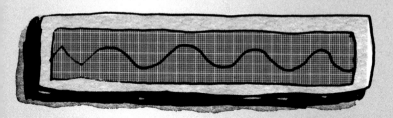

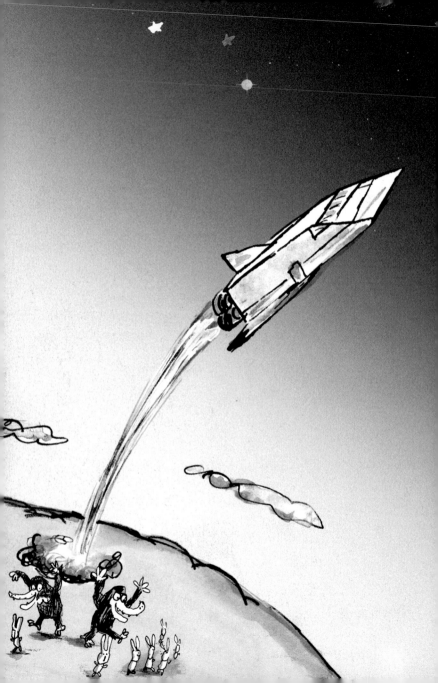

'You're invincible, aren't you? Just do it!'

There was a roaring sound and the floor began to tip. Tony could feel that they had already taken off.

'Returning to planet Earth at super-duper speed. Emergency landing procedures activated. Please take your seat, Master Spears . . . IMMEDIATELY!'

As Tony jumped into his seat he felt himself squeezed right back into it. He was travelling back to Earth, back to his house.

5. EMERGENCY LANDING!

On the screen Tony could see planet Earth growing rapidly in size like an inflating beach ball. He threw his hands over his face and then suddenly they were zooming over rooftops, before dropping like a stone into one of them, which had opened up like a jack in the box.

'Emergency descent thrusters activated.'

Everything was shaking like a skateboard on rough ground, until with a crumpling thump, everything was still.

'TOUCHDOWN.'

Tony leapt from his seat.

'Thanks, Computer. I've got to go. Bye!'

'Master Spears, before you exit do you want take your communicator with you?'

'My what?'

'Your communicator.'

Beside the switches controlling the airlock and outer hatch, a small panel had opened.

Inside the recess there was what looked like a digital watch on a little clear plastic display stand. The recess glowed in a green light that pulsed in time with the computer's voice.

'Look, I haven't got time for this—'

'Exactly, Tony; although its primary function is for you to stay in contact with me, it also has as many as twenty-six other modes including: Remote viewing and flight control. Biostatistics analysis and chronological time keeping . . .'

'Wait,' said Tony 'Chronological … That means time, doesn't it? You mean I can use it to tell the time?'

'Certainly, Master Spears. It can measure and manipulate any time units in the universe,

though it is capable of much —'

'Great,' said Tony. 'I'll take it. I need a new watch.

'Goodbye Computer,' yelled Tony again as he rushed down the gangplank back into the hyper-lift and into his kitchen.

Tony weaved his way back through the boxes to the lounge and leapt onto the sofa. He had just landed with a thump when he heard his mum's key in the door.

'Hi, Tony, I'm home. Sorry I'm late.'

She looked tired after a long day at her new job, and was carrying heavy bags of shopping. But then her tone of voice changed.

'Tony! Look at the state of the kitchen! How many times have I told you to tidy up after yourself?'

Tony crept off the sofa and went through to look at the kitchen. There were a few cupboard doors open here and there, and a few pots and pans spilling out onto the floor, but considering the whole room had just been transformed from a hyper-lift-link to an interstellar spaceship that had just performed an emergency landing, he didn't think it looked too bad.

'Um, sorry, Mum,' he said, hastily wiping some galactic biscuit from his mouth.

That night in bed Tony lay mulling over the day's events. It had all happened so fast that he hadn't had time to think through any of it.

First there was his day at his new school. As if that hadn't been difficult enough he had come back to his new house to discover that it had a spaceship underneath its kitchen, one that was invincible and capable of zooming through space, to the moon and to undiscovered planets like Xo49p, where he had made friends with the fuzzy Squggles who had saved his life. He could hardly bear to think about what had happened next. Those poor Squggles. He wished there was something he could do to make amends …

Why is this happening to me? thought Tony to himself. Is it really happening, or is it some kind of dream?

It seemed completely impossible but it felt real.

Tony had no idea how long he had been asleep when he was awoken by a strange noise. The house was dark and he guessed it was very early in the morning. There shouldn't have been any noises.

'Squeek.' There it was again.

It seemed to be coming from his cupboard …

'Squeeeeek.'

Tony tiptoed out of bed and slowly creaked the cupboard doors open.

It took several seconds for Tony to get used to the sight of a large pink fuzzy Squggle standing amongst his school clothes. It looked at Tony with its big eyes and then said, or telepathically said,

'Yes, it's me, Plumpy. Oh, Tony, please help me. I'm so scared!'

6. STOWAWAYS

'Plumpy! What are you doing here?'

But before Plumpy had time to reply, Tony's communicator burst into life,

'Master Spears, I would advise you to come to the ship immediately. We have a situation of some urgency that requires your attention.'

Looking at his bedroom window, Tony could see dawn creeping through the curtains.

Very quietly, he went downstairs clutching Plumpy, who was making little nervous chirping noises.

After activating the kitchen hyper-lift with the secret button, he was soon back inside the *Invincible*'s control room. The computer was right, thought Tony. It was easier the second time round. On board there were lights flashing, and beeping noises coming from almost every surface.

'Computer,' said Tony. 'Plumpy has stowed away and he's HERE on Earth! We must take

him back immediately, before anyone finds out.'

'I am aware of this, Tony, but there is a more pressing issue. Plumpy was not the only one to make it on board the *Invincible* before take-off. A Gatorilla managed to cling to the outer hull and was also brought here to planet Earth. It is currently somewhere in your house. Tony, do you remember what a Gatorilla is?'

'Yes, I do! Where is it now?'

'I'm afraid I cannot track the Gatorilla as it has gone beyond the *Invincible*'s special landing hangar, and due to the large amounts of shielding needed to protect your kitchen from the *Invincible*'s super-mega thrusters, my scanners cannot go beyond its limits.'

'Oh no! Well … is the Gatorilla on board?'

Tony could feel that he was sweating more than usual.

'No.'

'Phew. Right, Computer, close the bulkhead doors immediately, and all other doors and windows.'

'Bulkhead doors closed.'

'Computer, prepare for lift-off. We have to find that Gatorilla before it starts eating people!'

'I'm afraid that is impossible, Master Spears. During our emergency landing the spaceship's dilithium crystals became damaged, and we cannot take off until they are repaired.'

Now Tony began to feel very scared. He walked around the control room double-checking that all the doors and windows of the *Invincible* were shut. He felt numb all over. What was he to do? Somewhere out there was a Gatorilla. As long as he stayed inside the

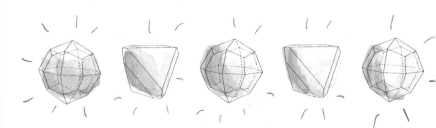

Invincible he would be safe, but his family and friends would not. And what about the other people in the town? The Gatorilla might eat them too. He couldn't let that happen. He had to do something …

He sat down in the command chair and after a while said, 'Computer, can you advise how to proceed?'

'Master Spears, firstly I would advise fixing the *Invincible*'s systems as soon as possible.

'Secondly I would capture the Gatorilla within the *Invincible*'s cargo hold, where, due to the ship's invincible-ness, he can be contained safely before, thirdly, returning Plumpy and the Gatorilla to planet Xo49p.'

The computer continued, 'It is likely that due to its size the Gatorilla is having trouble

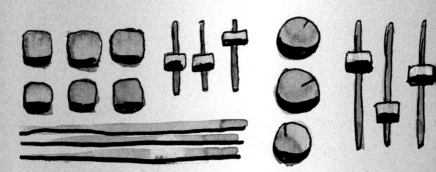

getting used to planet Earth. It may take him a number of days before he can move about. He has most likely found a safe place to hibernate, until he is able to hunt efficiently.'

'That's good. So at least I have a small amount of time.'

Tony could feel himself beginning to think clearly again.

'OK, Computer, you said I can repair the dilithium crystals. How?'

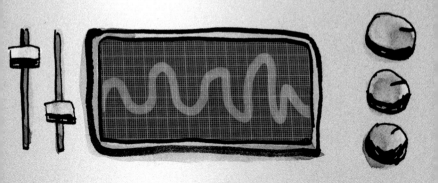

'I estimate repairing the *Invincible* to flightworthy conditions will require the following parts:

A cotton reel.

A cardboard toilet roll.

Some pins.

Sellotape.

And 215 grams of silver.'

Before Tony could say anything else, Plumpy explained.

'Tony, the *Invincible* has obviously been designed using things found throughout the multiverse, so it can be easily repaired.'

Plumpy. For a moment Tony had forgotten about him.

'And yes, Tony, of course I will help you, but we need to move fast.'

Gingerly Tony opened the bulkhead doors and together Plumpy and Tony tiptoed out from the safety of the *Invincible* and down the gangplank, looking over their shoulders every couple of paces ...

7. REPAIRS

After exiting the hyper-lift into his kitchen Tony set to work. It was 7.15 a.m. on Thursday morning. His mum had Thursday mornings off. If he was lucky she might lie in, but even so he would only have an hour or so before he had to go to school.

'Plumpy, can you use your amazingly large ears to listen out for the Gatorilla? If you hear even the slightest growl in this house, or anywhere at all, please let me know.'

'OK, good idea, Tony. Not hearing anything yet.'

Plumpy started revolving his head round and round on his shoulders like a radar, whilst Tony began collecting things.

Right, what was on the list? A cotton
reel. Hmm … a cotton reel. Where had he seen
a cotton reel? Yes, that was it, in the kitchen
drawer with the damp matches … Cotton reel;
got it! Perhaps this wouldn't be so difficult
after all!

Rushing around the house as quickly and quietly as he could, opening boxes and cupboards, it didn't take Tony too long to assemble most of the things on the list. The cardboard toilet roll proved a bit troublesome so Tony had unravel the toilet roll from the bathroom, remove the tube and roll it back up as best he could, making it look like there was still a tube inside. Hopefully his mum wouldn't notice.

The only thing that he couldn't find was silver. They didn't have any in the house, and as far as he knew it was expensive to buy, and even if he knew where to buy it, Tony didn't have any money. But in any case it was now time for school. He could hear his mum stirring upstairs. The question was what to do with Plumpy.

'Oh please don't leave me here, Tony. I think it's best we stay together. Remember,

I have the best ears on the planet. If that Gatorilla makes so much as a peep, I'll be the first one to hear it.'

As Plumpy refused to go in Tony's school bag (and in any case he was far too big for it), the only thing was for Tony to carry him. 'Well, I guess you kind of look like a toy anyway.

'Crumbs, Plumpy, you're much heavier than you look!' He wolfed down some cereal, gave his mum a quick kiss goodbye and left the house.

On the way to school, Tony noticed some other children in the purple, green and gold uniform of St John's, standing outside Mr Gumbrell's shop eating sweets. Tony slowed his walk right down and tried to hide behind a parked car, but they had already seen him.

To begin with they looked over with friendly smiles, obviously remembering him as 'the new kid', but when they saw Plumpy (well, he was BRIGHT pink and fluffy) the sniggers started. The sniggers continued all the way along that street, the next street and by

131

the time Tony arrived at school, he felt his face was as pink as Plumpy's fur. Tony wanted to run back home, back to the *Invincible* where he could close all the doors and windows, be on his own and be safe. But he couldn't. He had to repair the *Invincible* and capture that Gatorilla. All he needed was some silver, and he wasn't going to find that shut inside a spaceship on his own.

'Come along now, children,' said their teacher, Mr Simpson. 'Quickly, quickly. Coats on the pegs, bags in your cupboards and,

Tony– as he spoke to Tony his face softened, 'Ah yes, Tony. It's awfully sweet to bring your toy to school, but I'm afraid it will have to stay here with your bags. No toys allowed in school. Perhaps at lunchtime I'll let you have a little play with it.'

Once everyone was sitting at their desks the day could begin as usual, with Mr Simpson reciting the school notices before lessons.

'… And finally, as I'm sure you are all aware, the annual "award for the most outstanding pupil" reaches its climax tomorrow when the winner will be announced.

'With this in mind, normal lessons will be suspended for these next two days, and will be replaced with some special tasks where some all-important extra points can be won.

'So this morning we shall be doing art,

with triple points going to the most creative and imaginative artworks.

'Art will then be followed by a special test, designed to see how much you have learnt this term. Again, triple points for every right answer.

'And finally tomorrow morning is Sports Morning, when we will have races and other sporting activities, with bonus points going to the winners. This will be followed immediately by the prize-giving afternoon, when the winner will be announced.

'But before we start, to help give you all
an incentive, I have in my hand THE PRIZE!

'Yes, this is the cup that will be awarded to the pupil who has won the most points overall!'

'Oooohhh,' went Tony's class.

The cup was an impressive sight. It was bright, shiny, silvery and—

'Yes, Tony you're right. I have just telepathically spoken to your computer, which has analysed the cup. It IS made of silver, and it weighs 550 grams.'

550 grams of silver, thought Tony. More than enough to repair the ship's dilithium crystals, capture that Gatorilla and send it back to Xo49p.

I HAVE TO to win that award!

But it isn't going to be easy.

8. ART AND GRAFT

The art class started immediately after that and Tony was pleased. He enjoyed art, so this could be a chance to get some extra points. He collected some paper and paint, and set to work immediately.

Around him, his classmates were busily working away, with Mr Simpson walking around, occasionally giving bits of advice and encouragement. There was a clock ticking on the wall.

'Ah, Tony, I can see that you've been very busy. Let's have a look at what you've been painting.

'Ahem, Tony, yes, well, this is very … imaginative …' said Mr Simpson with his voice trailing off.

'This looks like the little toy rabbit you brought in, but what does this strange-toothed face here represent in your picture?'

'That's a Gatorilla,' said Tony. 'They are HUGE animals, like a cross between a gorilla and an alligator. They are dangerous! If you or anyone else in the class sees one you must run away IMMEDIATELY. Before it snaps and chomps you in its jaws … And it's not imaginitive, it's REAL!'

'Um yes, Tony. Thank you, dear.' And although Mr Simpson looked somewhat bemused, Tony thought he quite liked the painting.

During lunch, whilst the other children went through their school books in readiness for the test, Tony began planning what he would do. He wasn't at all hopeful about getting any extra points here. Because he had joined so late in the term, he had missed almost all the lessons, so what hope did he have of knowing any of the answers?

He devised a plan which went something like this.

TONY'S PLAN

1. Read question.
2. Ask computer answer.

3. Computer tells answer (coz it seems to know everything)

4. WRITE ANSWER!

5. GET FULL POINTS, EASY PEASY!!!

It seemed foolproof but in practice things proved a little more troublesome.

The children filed in to the classroom and sat at their desks. On each desk was a sheet of questions.

'Right,' said Mr Simpson. 'Remember this is just for fun but it's still a test so no talking. And no cheating! The test starts NOW. Good luck!'

This is great, thought Tony. What can possibly go wrong?

The first question was to do with Italy.

Tony whispered quietly into his communicator, 'What food do Italians like to eat?'

And he sat and waited for the response, but nothing came.

He repeated the question a little bit louder, but still nothing.

'Computer, are you there?'

'Yes, I am here, Tony.'

'Then why didn't you answer? I asked you a question.'

'I am aware of that, Tony, but I am unable to answer because you are in a test, and it would be against the rules of the test to collude with you. I clearly heard Mr Simpson say, "no cheating".'

'But I need to cheat to win. I'll never be able to win the cup otherwise.'

'I am sure you can win on your own merits, Tony, and in any case, it is impossible for me to help you: my justice circuits would not allow it. You will have to do this on your own.'

Tony was about to shout something back to the communicator when Mr Simpson bellowed, 'Hey! Anyone else talking will be disqualified!'

Tony sat back down. He thought back to painting of the Gatorilla, and then to his mum, and all the other mums of the town. He had no choice. He would have to do this on his own.

'What is it people like to eat in Italy …?' he mused.

The test took the rest of the afternoon and then it was home time. Tony was sweating by the end of it. Dredging up everything he knew about anything, and trying to puzzle out things he didn't know anything about. It was hard work. But despite doing his absolute best, when collecting his bag, coat and Plumpy to go home he began to feel despondent. He had probably got a few more points in the test, and in the art class, but what was the point when tomorrow was Sports Morning? Tony was definitely not very good at sports.

Suddenly Plumpy interrupted his thoughts

'Tony, I have located the Gatorilla. It is HERE in the school building. Asleep in the caretaker's cupboard!'

9. THE CARETAKER'S CUPBOARD...

The pupils of St John's were not meant to enter the caretaker's cupboard. There was no sign saying so, and no teachers had ever told them so, it was just one of those corners of the school that was out of bounds.

There was a key poking out of the lock. Tony nervously turned it, opened the door and went in. It was much larger than he expected,

and was filled with mop buckets, big cans of detergent and other cleaning products. There was a dusty window covered in cobwebs, lots of tools hanging against one wall, but definitely no Gatorilla.

He looked questioningly at Plumpy, who was looking up at the ceiling.

Following Plumpy's eyes upward he saw why. There, curled up amongst the hot water pipes and the fluorescent lights was a huge, hairy, toothy, clawed Gatorilla, who thankfully was fast asleep.

'C'mon,' whispered Tony. 'We've got to move fast. If this thing wakes up here, there's going to be trouble.'

Tony pointed his communicator at the slumbering beast.

'Computer,' he whispered into his communicator. 'I have located the Gatorilla. Are you ready to teleport?'

'Well done, Tony. I am currently charging my teleporter-zapper-system but due to the damage to my dilithium crystals, teleportation cannot occur for at least sixteen hours. You

will have to keep the Gatorilla contained until then.'

Tony blanched. Sixteen hours! That would not be until tomorrow morning. Anything could happen! Perhaps he could do it before Sports Morning the following day?

Tony tiptoed out of the room with Plumpy, closed the door and, as quietly as he could, turned the key in the lock. 'Well, I guess that will have to do for now.'

Back home there was lots to prepare before school the next day. Firstly there was the teleporting and repairing to talk over with the computer.

Once on board the *Invincible* he noticed things were different. It was quite gloomy, and the whole ship was lit by dim red lighting.

'Computer, can you turn the lights up, please. I can't see a thing.'

'I'm afraid that is not possible, Tony. I must charge the teleporter-zapper-system with what little power I have left before I am repaired, so I must economise my power use wherever possible.

'Teleporting a large object like a Gatorilla into my secure hold will use up almost all my reserves, and once teleported, I can only contain him for as long as my power holds out. If my power fails completely, I will be unable to prevent him escaping.'

The computer then showed him how to aim his communicator, and which button to press. At least that seems straight-forward enough, thought Tony. After that it was back to his room to prepare his sports kit ready for the next day.

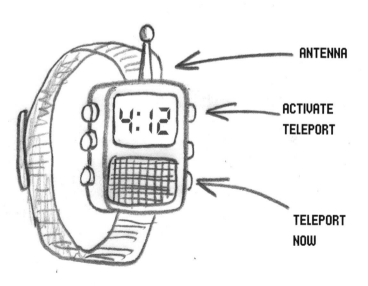

ANTENNA

ACTIVATE TELEPORT

TELEPORT NOW

As Tony passed his mum on the stairs, she looked at him with concern.

'Are you worried about the sports day tomorrow, Tony? I'm hoping to come along if I can get time off work,' she said.

There was so much going on in Tony's head, he thought it would burst, but he couldn't tell her about any of it, and even if he could, he wouldn't know where to start, so instead he gave her a big hug.

As she put her arms around him she said,

'Just do your best; you can't do any better than that.'

And then it was time for bed. After
turning off his light Tony ran through the plan
a few more times in his head, before pulling
up his covers and whispering goodnight to
Plumpy, who had taken to sleeping by his feet.
They both needed their rest. Tomorrow was
going to be a busy day.

10. LAST CHANCE

When the school gates opened the next morning, Tony was the first pupil through them.

'My, you're keen today, said Mr Simpson. He was dressed in his PE kit: red tracksuit and trousers with a whistle around his neck.

'Um, well, you know. The early bird catches the …' But Tony couldn't remember the phrase.

'Award?' finished Mr Simpson.

'Yes, that's it, the early bird catches the award,' said Tony. 'This is my mascot. Can I leave it on the sports field later?'

And Tony was off.

He headed to the caretaker's cupboard first.

'Plumpy,' he whispered. 'Set your ears on high alert. Let me know if that Gatorilla moves so much as a muscle.'

As he neared the cupboard door, Tony got ready to press the teleportation button on his communicator, whilst his other hand roved towards the door handle.

He was just about to open it when Plumpy said, 'Stop, Tony, something's wrong. I can't hear him!'

CARETAKER

169

'But that's good, isn't it?' said Tony.

'Not exactly. By that I mean I can't hear him AT ALL, not even snoring. Tony, I don't think he's in there any more!'

But before they got a chance to find out the school bell rang. 'Brrrring!'

And all the children in the busy playground began to line into their classrooms.

'Right, everyone!' shouted Mr Simpson. 'PE kits on and straight to the field. Let the games begin! Tony, away from that door. This way, please!'

In a flurry of activity, school uniforms were discarded and sports kits were put on, but as Tony and all the other children walked from the classroom towards the sports field, Tony noticed something very strange about the canteen.

All the windows were broken, and one of them was actually missing, leaving a gaping hole in the building. Through the hole he could see the large pans used by the school dinner cooks thrown around and bent out of shape like soft cheese. The headmaster stood nearby talking to a policeman in uniform.

'I just don't understand it. Why would anyone do something like this? These vandals are so thoughtless.'

'Yes, I see it too, Tony,' whispered Plumpy. 'I think that the Gatorilla has woken up ... hungry!'

On the field, a few parents were assembled. Tony placed Plumpy on the sidelines with them, and arranged his ears as best he could, to give Plumpy the best chance of hearing in all directions.

'Let me know if you hear anything,' whispered Tony as he set him down. 'We might have to act fast if that Gatorilla appears.'

Tony's first event was the long jump. Standing on the starting line, wiggling his legs like he'd seen atheletes do on TV he could hear his classmates cheering, 'Go, Tony!' And suddenly, in the fraction of a second before he started running, it occurred to him that they all knew his name. Then he was off, sprinting down the track.

In a few quick strides he got to the jumping line and just as his leading foot hit it, he caught sight of the Gatorilla in the distance.

It was standing on the roof of Mr Gumbrell's shop beating its chest like something out of a King Kong film. Tony jumped, throwing himself forward with all his might, finally landing in the sand with a thump, but he didn't stop there. Keeping his legs whirling, spraying sand everywhere, he sprinted out of the sandpit towards the shop.

On the way he passed the start of the 200-metre hurdles just as their starting gun went off. Tony quickly sped out past the leaders, jumping hurdle after hurdle, breaking

179

the winning tape (to more cheers) and then hurdling over the school fence into the street where Mr Gumbrell's shop was.

The Gatorilla was not on the roof any more, but judging from the way in which the roof had been removed and thrown across the road, it was inside.

Tony ran through the shop door, almost pinging the customer bell off its hinges. There were tins, toilet rolls and boxes everywhere. It looked like someone had turned the shop upside down.

The Gatorilla was sitting hunched up by the sweet counter, grabbing sweets, and the whole shop smelt of something familiar. What was it now … Yes that was it … bubblegum! The Gatorilla was picking up packets of it, chewing and chewing, and chewing and chewing, before gulping down the whole lot, paper packets and all. Behind him was Mr Gumbrell with a broom, shouting, 'Back! Get OUT! SHOO! Don't you dare eat my stock!'

By now the Gatorilla had emptied nearly the whole shelf of Bubblyummmagum in all

183

different flavours.

Tony shouted into his communicator, 'I am with the Gatorilla! Computer, are you ready to teleport?'

'Raising energy profile now,' replied the computer. As it spoke its voice became lower, slower and more distant and crackly.

'Tony, my power is draining much more than I feared. Teleportation will be possible in approximately 30 seconds. But that will drain my emergency power totally. A second attempt will not be possible.

'28 seconds.

'27 seconds.

'26 seconds.'

By now the Gatorilla had chewed
and gulped down the entire shelf of
Bubblyummagum. He turned round to face
Tony and Mr Gumbrell, and roared, showing
rows and rows of sharp teeth.

Then Tony had an idea.

'Mr Gumbrell, have you any more
Bubblyummagum in your shop?'

'Yes, in the back room.'

The Gatorilla roared again, this time in a much more menacing fashion, and began moving towards Mr Gumbrell.

Mr Gumbrell waved his broom in its face.

'Stop that! You haven't paid for that! You are STEALING!' he shouted.

The Gatorilla picked up the broom, with Mr Gumbrell on the other end of it, and hurled it across the room.

Mr Gumbrell landed upside down in the greetings card stand, with a thump. He was knocked out cold.

Meanwhile Tony had made his way to the back room, returning with as much Bubblyummagum as he could carry. He started hurling big boxes of it at the Gatorilla, with the Gatorilla catching them in his open jaws, before chewing them and swallowing them whole.

'Computer, how long now?

'13 seconds . . .

'10 seconds . . .

'7 seconds . . .'

By now Tony was out of Bubblyummagum.
The Gatorilla roared with anger, beating
his chest and leaping towards Tony, talons
outstretched.

'3 seconds . . .

'Now, Tony!'

Tony was knocked flat to the ground by
the force of its leap.

There was a blinding flash, and the smell
of toasted marshmallows.

'Are you all right, son?'

Lying flat on his back Tony blinked a few times and then opened his eyes to see a man in a large hat leaning over him. Tony quickly realised he was a policeman.

'Um, yes I'm fine, but I need to get back to school.'

There were lots of other people in the shop too: the fire brigade; an ambulance crew, who were putting a bandage around Mr Gumbrell's head; a team of people with large nets and the words ZOO KEEPERS written on their backs; some other men and ladies with jackets that said RSPCA; and several members of the local press.

Everyone was shouting at once.

Mr Gumbrell was telling the zoo keepers that several animals had escaped from their zoo and run amok through his shop. Mrs Gumbrell was telling the police that some armed robbers dressed as animals had broken into their shop. Several other bystanders were saying how a giant furry eagle had removed the roof of the shop and people shouldn't be allowed to keep dangerous birds as pets, especially if they can remove the roofs of shops.

'It was a gorilla that escaped from the zoo!'

'No, a crocodile! In fact, several crocodiles!'

'An eagle!'

'So about these robbers, Mr Gumbrell,' said the policeman, scratching his head. 'Were they dressed as crocodiles or gorillas?'

It was all very confusing. The only thing everyone was agreed on was that it was a young schoolboy, dressed in the St John's sports colours, that had saved the day. But amidst all the confusion, the hero schoolboy had sidled out of the shop and disappeared …

11. FINALE

There was no time to lose. Jumping back over the fence, and running across the sports fields, Tony tried to use his communicator to contact the computer but heard nothing back. This didn't suprise him. Teleporting the Gatorilla to its cargo hold must have drained its power entirely. How long the Gatorilla would stay there Tony wasn't sure, but he knew it wouldn't be long.

He needed to get that silver, and soon.

In the hall, all the children and teachers were already assembled for the awards ceremony. Amongst them, he caught sight of his mum. In her arms she held Plumpy; she lifted him up and smiled at Tony. At the back of the stage was a big banner which said 'St John's, Raising The Standard of Excellence'. The headteacher stood up and addressed the hall.

'Well, thank you for all coming here this afternoon to help us celebrate this year's "most outstanding pupil award".

It's been a busy term, and a very exciting last couple of days, but all the points have been added up, and I am pleased to announce that we have a winner. Can Bertrand Russell please take to the stage.'

There was a huge round of applause as Bertrand walked onto the stage.

Tony's heart sank into his stomach. That was it. He hadn't won the award. He didn't have the silver he needed to repair the ship's dilithium crystals. Any moment now the

Invincible's batteries would drain completely and the Gatorilla would be free again. It had all been in vain.

After the applause had died down the headteacher continued, 'I'm sure you will join me in congratulating all the pupils this year, who have all worked very hard, but in addition to first prize, this year we have added a new prize to the ceremony, for the pupil who has made the most progress, and tried hardest in all events. Please stand up, Tony Spears.'

Tony was stunned. He stumbled to his feet and made his way forward. In the background he could hear the school cheering him whilst the headteacher handed him a small silver plate, with 'Tony Spears' engraved into it.

He took his seat and went over to find his mum, who was still clutching Plumpy, wiping a tear from her eye. 'Oh, Tony, I'm so proud of you. I knew you could do it.' And she gave him a big hug.

'C'mon, I'll take you home.'

12. EPILOGUE

It was lovely getting a ride home in Mum's car. Still in his sports kit, sitting in the back cuddling Plumpy, Tony suddenly realised how tired he was. But his work wasn't done yet; there were still a few things to do.

After his mum dropped him off, he made his way straight to the *Invincible*. On board there were no lights at all, except for a single pulsing glow in the centre of the computer's

screen. Making his way to the engine room
Tony carefully placed all the items he had
collected in the correct places, finishing
with the small silver plate he had won that
afternoon. He took one last look at it before

placing it in the repair slot, closing the lid and pressing the 'repair' button. Within seconds all the lights came on again and the computer began going through its checks.

Tony breathed a sigh of relief when he saw it display **'Cargo bay secured'**. And finally,

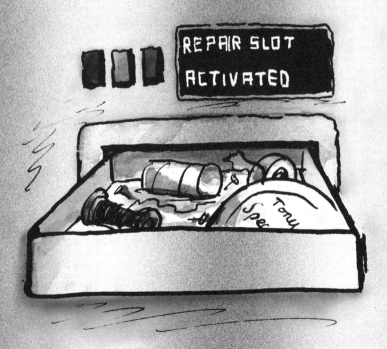

'Repairs complete.

'Checks complete.

'*Invincible* ready for launch.'

During the journey back to planet Xo49p Plumpy and Tony talked. Plumpy was full of praise for Tony. Tony was full of praise for Plumpy, and together they formed a plan.

As Tony now knew, the Gatorillas LOVED bubblegum. (Well, the whole of planet Xo49p smelt of it!) So once they landed, after a quick visit to their 'Centre for Science', the Squggles were soon producing vast quantities of it in all different colours and flavours, which were then transported to the surface.

As Plumpy and Tony expected, the Gatorillas immediately fell upon the piles of bubblegum, munching and chewing away to their hearts' content, and quickly turned from scary-angry Gatorillas, into lazy-half-asleep-

wouldn't-hurt-a-fly Gatorillas.

'They sure do like their bubblegum,' said Plumpy. 'It totally changes their mood. They become as playful as pussy cats as long as their jaws are full of it.'

'Well, everyone gets a bit grumpy when they get hungry,' remarked Tony.

'I can't thank you enough for all you've done for our planet, Tony.'

'Don't mention it, Plumpy. Remember, you've helped me too, in more ways that I can say.'

And so with one last big hug, Tony bade farewell to his pink furry telepathic friend, and as the *Invincible* zoomed its way back to planet Earth in time for Tony's tea, we are left with this scene on the now peaceful and tranquil planet Xo49p, just one of the two billion planets in the universe capable of supporting human life.

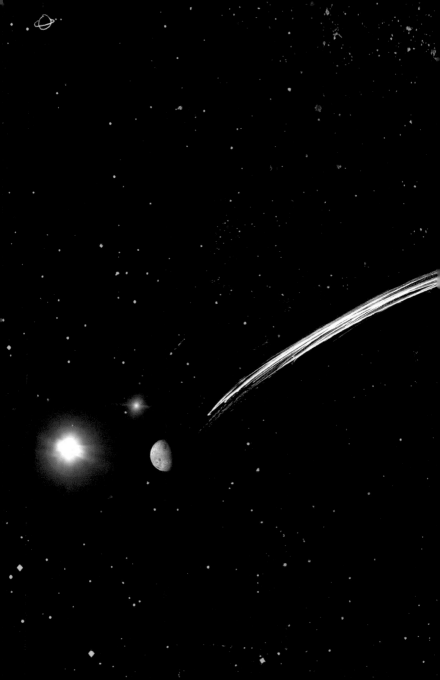

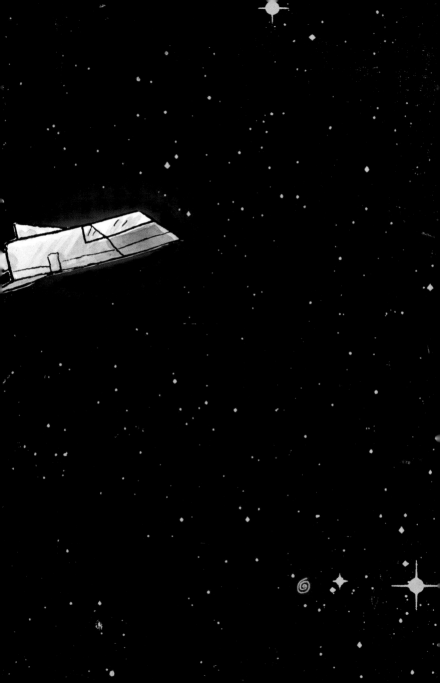

COSMIC QUESTIONS AND ANSWERS WITH

Neal Layton

⭐ **If you had to have a pet Gatorilla in your home, how would you take care of it?**

⭐ I would walk it twice a day and brush it and comb it, but above all, make sure it was well fed!

⭐ **Did you have a pet when you were younger?**

⭐ I had lots of pets. Garden snails, a caterpillar that turned into a butterfly. I also tried to keep ants but they escaped. And we had a cat.

⭐ **What one thing do you think is essential to take to space?**

⭐ A map of the stars to get back home, and a spare pair of socks.

⭐ **When you close your eyes at night, do you see planet Xo49p?**

⭐ I don't so much see it, as smell it – pink bubblegum ... Mmmmm!

⭐ **Planet Xo49p smells of pink bubblegum. What do you think would be a great smell for planet Earth?**

🌟 Maybe chocolate? Although I did work in a chocolate factory once and it is possible to go off that smell!

⭐ **What will Tony do next?**

🌟 Tony will have lots more cosmic adventures, you can be sure of that! The universe is a very BIG place – who knows what else is out there …